MW01278618

DARKSIDE SEATTLE:
MECHANIC

DARKSIDE SEATTLE:
MECHANIC

L.E. FRENCH

Published by Clockwork Dragon Books

clockworkdragon.net

First printing, January 2018

ISBN: 978-1-944334-23-9

For the real Chimi.

CHAPTER 1

Whirring from my power drill echoed inside the ravaged carcass of an older model Ford hovercar's engine cavity. Sweat soaked my shirt and dripped from my forehead, caused by the spotlight blaring over my shoulder. The light passed through the empty space to the inspection pit below the car where its transmission rested on a wheeled cart, waiting for me to use the pulley system to drag it up to ground level.

My nephew, Mateo, used a standard shop power drill with a screwdriver bit to remove the stereo system. This piece of shit didn't seem worth the effort we put into dismantling it, but what Mead First, the gang controlling the area, wanted, they got.

Mateo straightened and popped out his foam earplugs. "I'm ready to call it a night." He spoke Spanish like we always did whenever no customers were around. The car's boxy stereo in hand, he slid through the gaping hole where the passenger door had once been.

I raised my right arm, the one that had been replaced by a cybernetic prosthetic, and issued a mental command, causing the protective cover on my finger to slide over the drill bit. Once, I'd forgotten and broke the tip. Once.

Out came the fourth and final part of the computer brain. The gang's car thieves had already disabled the 'net link, so I could take my time with it. We still had a deadline to chop this thing, though. If not for Mead First's demands, Mateo wouldn't have come to work at all. When he got home, I had no doubt his wife would make him pay for abandoning her with their first baby only six days after the birth.

The visual overlay on my eyesight provided by my government-mandated cranial implant reported the time as 23:12, five hours after we'd closed the shop for the day. "Go home," I said with a shrug, popping out my own earplugs. "I got this. It'll be done by dawn."

Mateo set the stereo aside and crossed his arms to glare, his dark eyes reminding me too much of his father. "It can wait until morning."

"Sure." I shrugged and nodded toward the nearby

engine block, dangling from chains attached to a crane anchored to the concrete floor of the repair bay. All four tires and rims had been stacked to the side, along with the headlights and taillights.

"The hardest parts are done already anyway," I said. "It's just details now."

He huffed and opened his mouth to say something else.

Bright light flashed across the front windows. We both cringed from it.

"Fuck," Mateo spat. "Big Chimi said we had three days, not two."

I shrugged. "Go out there and tell them it's not done. They can take what's chopped already if they want and come back for the rest tomorrow night. Big Chimi's not a complete dick."

Mateo grumbled under his breath and stalked to the door.

I turned my attention back to the car. If Mead First had stepped up their deadline for some reason, I figured they should find me working, not sitting with my thumb up my ass. At my mental command, the drill bit in my finger shifted to a Phillips-head screwdriver bit, and I bent to remove screws.

My visual display flashed with a message notification from Mateo. I opened and read it.

[MateoAcosta: It's not the gang.]

With a whisper of thought, I composed a response. The idea of who it might be put a sour taste in my mouth, and I grimaced.

[IsabellaAcosta: Cops?]

[MateoAcosta: No.]

Mateo backed into the garage with his hands up. Two muscle-bound men followed him, one holding a gun pointed at him and the other swaggering. They wore dark tactical suits with matching, full-head cycle helmets that covered their faces with dark plastic. Both sported dual pistol holsters, multiple knife sheaths, and bulging pockets.

Beyond the borders of Darkside Seattle, cops would never let them ride—or walk, for that matter—like that. Our shop clung to the south fringe of DeeSeat, where they'd have to choose their path with care to avoid arrest.

"Who's this?" The man not holding a gun on Mateo spoke with an obvious voice modulator.

"One of my employees," Mateo said.

The man drew a gun and pointed it at me. "Bitch,

leave."

I stood and made sure the chrome on my arm flashed in the light. "Go fuck yourself," I snapped. This family didn't leave anyone alone with strangers. We'd all learned that lesson the hard way.

Our new friend stood still for a second, then he put up his gun and laughed. "Fine. Stay, but keep your mouth shut, bitch."

No matter how scared I wasn't, I knew when to shut it and let the boys believe they'd won. I retracted my power drill and crossed my arms.

"We need a cow chip," the asshole said.

"I don't have one," Mateo said. He'd never been as bold or brassy as his father. Diego would've asked if the men saw any cows around, and he would've insulted them while doing it.

"No shit. You're going to get one for us. We'll pay a fair market rate for it."

Mateo lowered his hands. He turned to check with me.

I quirked an eyebrow. The first time someone had come to shake down the shop, a long time ago, my father had talked over his decision to bow to the inevitable with Diego and me. We fought when we had to fight and backed down when we didn't.

That didn't mean we had to let them walk all over us.

"Are you fucking nuts?" I said. "We don't do illegal shit like that here."

"What do you call that?" The asshole gestured with his gun at our chop job.

"What do we call what?" Mateo said with a nonchalant shrug. He jerked a thumb over his shoulder at the car husk. "That's perfectly legal."

The asshole barked another laugh. "Sure it is. Then you can produce the paperwork for it." Instead of giving Mateo a chance to trot out his well-rehearsed citation of the laws to make our illegal activities sound legit, he sprang forward and pressed the barrel of his gun against Mateo's head.

"Knock it off," I said. These fuckers didn't deserve to get what they wanted, but as my father used to say, sometimes you have to let God handle the assholes. "I can get you a fucking cow chip."

"I'll bet you can. You'd probably go run out and snatch one from a fire truck, though. We need one from a cop car."

I stared at him. He was right, of course. My cousin worked for the fire department. He'd help me figure out a way to get it done without endangering his job. Getting one from a police vehicle, on the other hand, I had no idea how to do. "What makes you think we can get a cow chip out of a cop car without Seattle PD Dispatch noticing and shutting it off? We're mechanics, not thieves."

The asshole laughed again, this time dark and sinister. He nodded to his buddy. The other guy wrapped his meaty, gloved hand around Mateo's arm.

"Here's how things are. You have one day to get us a live cow chip from a cop car, or we kill him."

I froze. Blood drained from my face. "You're bluffing." The words tumbled out before I could stop them.

"No, I'm really not. A day from now. We'll call it midnight. Meet us in the lot for the old stadium."

"What the fuck," Mateo said.

The silent asshole yanked Mateo's arm. When he resisted, the other asshole pressed his gun barrel harder against Mateo's forehead. They dragged him toward the door.

"I don't know how to get one out of a cop car," I said, frantic for any reason to get these guys to leave without taking

Mateo.

"You have a day to figure it out."

The two men hauled Mateo out of the garage. My nephew looked at me, fear etched across his face. I didn't know what to do or where to go. How the fuck was I supposed to get what they wanted without getting arrested?

"Oh, and let's not have you following us." The asshole shot his gun.

The bang exploded in my ears, echoing off the walls. I felt an impact on my arm without comprehending it. They disappeared from sight with me still standing there, staring at the empty doorway. Blood stained my faded blue jumpsuit.

The bright lights retreated. My ears rang.

Pain reared its ugly head in the dark, empty garage. I panicked while I bled.

CHAPTER 2

My brain raced, trying to come up with a plan. If I knew where to find Mateo, I could kidnap him back. I didn't. If I had a cop friend, I could invite them over and do something horrible to get access to their car. I didn't.

I didn't even know where to find a stupid cow chip in a cop car, let alone remove it. We'd never chopped anything with one. Mead First had enough brains among them not to try jacking emergency vehicles or cop cars. Nothing like fucking with one of those to bring down a swarm of SWAT on your ass.

Out of desperation, I messaged Mateo.

[IsabellaAcosta: Where are they taking you?]

[IsabellaAcostaSystem: This account is currently unavailable and not accepting messages.]

They'd found a way to block his implant. Of course they had. Kidnapping didn't work if the victim could message for rescue. I spat some expletives and paced across the garage. The deadline for Mateo came after the deadline for the chop job. Which seemed like a stupid thing to think, but it popped into my head.

Did I have any possible way to convince Mateo's wife that something other than his abduction had happened? No. She saw through bullshit as easy as the Curandera. Rumor said she'd take the old woman's place someday.

My arm ached. Speaking of the Curandera, I'd been shot. Fucking god, I'd been shot. My arm wouldn't obey me. It dangled at my side, limp and useless. How did those fuckers expect me to do anything like this?

I clamped my metal cyberhand over the wound. That seemed like the right thing to do. When did I start crying? Tears dripped from my chin and snot ran from my nose.

"Get a grip, Bella. Get a fucking grip." I glanced at my fake hand, holding my arm. Giggles burst from my mouth. They turned to sobs and I wanted to hit something. Those two assholes would suffice, if I could find them.

Yeah, I'd show up at the stadium with a gun and those two fuckers would die.

No, I didn't know how to shoot. I didn't even have a gun. Besides, for all I knew, those tactical suits included ballistic armor. Then both Mateo and I would both die because I wanted to win.

I had to find a cop car, spend enough time with it to find the cow chip, and leave it the way I found it so no one realized I'd taken it. As a bonus, I got to fuck with a cop and make his life hell for a day or two. All those assholes deserved it.

Of course, I had to figure out the path from point A to point B. I had no idea how to get time with a cop car, let alone where to find the stupid chip inside one.

Someone else might have some ideas.

Wiping my face on the shoulder of my grease-stained jumpsuit, I pushed through the door and slammed it shut. The air tasted damp and metallic, promising rain before dawn.

My display flashed with a message from Mateo's wife. I ignored it to stagger through our small lot of cars waiting for attention. Soft light from strings of white Christmas bulbs mounted on poles guided me to the street. If the streetlights worked in our neighborhood, we'd take the strings down.

They didn't call it Darkside Seattle for no reason.

Our generator ran on alcohol and sweat. Since we'd worked so late, the battery would fail in another hour at most. Mateo had probably intended to keep attacking that car carcass until the power failed.

Once in a while, I wondered why no one ever came down here and bulldozed the whole area to make way for fancy high-rises or new warehouses. They could reconnect the electrical grid if they wanted. Something worthwhile could rise from the ashes of all this. Instead, the powerful let it fester.

Papa once told me it let them have a place they could contain everything undesirable so it didn't infect the rest of the city. No one had the power to stamp out poverty and crime, so keep someplace for it to proliferate. Like sweeping it under the rug.

The theory seemed reasonable to me.

The sky opened, drenching me in a downpour as I hurried through the darkness. I knew the route. The Curandera was my aunt. My mother's sister, and the only member of the family left around here with more years than me. Of the rest of the neighborhood, I could count all the people older than me on one hand.

At thirty-nine, I counted as an elder in our barrio.

Skirting the edge of DeeSeat, I stumbled for three blocks. Two and three story buildings loomed in the darkness. Flickering firelight danced on the uneven walls of a pile of rubble occupying a space between two apartment buildings.

Rain sluiced away my panic, leaving numbness in its wake. In one day, Mateo would die, and I couldn't stop it. I couldn't even feel my fingers.

The Curandera lived in a nice building, for the neighborhood. The concrete tenement's front door fit in its frame and unmolested glass filled the barred windows. Seattle kept it clean in its natural way, at least on the outside.

I pushed through the front door and hauled my ass up a flight of bare metal steps thick with the stench of bleach. Old-fashioned cameras, the only kind anyone had around here, whirred as they followed my progress to the second floor. At the landing, I had to stop and catch my breath. Water dripped off my boots and slid through the holes in the floor to plunk, plunk, plunk ten feet below.

Shivers started at the base of my neck and spread. I took it as a sign I needed to move. Hauling open the fire door meant letting go of my injured arm, but if I hadn't passed out yet, I didn't think I would. Thin, industrial carpet in a muddy shade of brown or red, or maybe orange, covered the hallway floor and walls. Round blobs of yellow light glowed from the popcorn ceiling.

At number twenty-three, I knocked and waited. Then I remembered the time. It always sat in my vision, but like everyone else, I'd learned to ignore it by the age of ten.

[IsabellaAcosta: Sorrybotherlatehurt.]

I re-read my message. The letters blurred together, just like the words. That wasn't supposed to happen. Implants sent their information straight to and from the brain. My eyelids drooped. I blinked hard.

The door opened. Aunt Catalina filled the space wearing the rattiest robe ever to grace her sturdy frame. She frowned at me, her face framed by a halo of gray-streaked black hair lit from behind.

Everything slid sideways. No, that was me. My cybered shoulder hit the doorjamb. Catalina reached for me.

CHAPTER 3

The next thing I knew, I lay on the Curandera's slab with bright light in my face. I cringed from the light with a groan. My arm throbbed. Warm weight held me down.

"I died." My voice cracked and creaked.

"You did not," Catalina said in Spanish. I heard her roll her eyes at me. "You passed out. Drink."

Something pressed against my lips. I opened my mouth for a straw and drank warm, minty water through it.

"Who shot you?"

Everything rushed back, including panic. I tried to sit up, but couldn't. Squinting, I saw Catalina holding me down with a firm hand on my chest.

"Settle down or you'll need another fake arm."

I stopped struggling and took a few deep breaths.

"Now, tell me who shot you."

"I don't know. They didn't show their faces." I told

her everything. In the middle, I started crying. She helped me sit up and held me close, like Mama used to do when I was little.

When I finished, she rocked me for a few minutes more. Then she said, "Do you think it was Mead First?"

Clinging to her, I tried to imagine Big Chimi or any of his people acting like those two men had. "No."

"No, it doesn't sound like them. Get some sleep, *chica*, then go see them in the morning."

"Go see them? Why?"

She pulled away so I could see her sad smile. "This happened on their turf, didn't it? Don't we all pay them for protection?"

I blinked at her like an idiot. "So?"

"So they didn't do a good job of protecting you and Mateo, did they?"

She shouldn't have had to spell that out for me. I should've come to that conclusion on my own. Maybe I would have after some sleep, but I didn't have time for sleep. My head felt fuzzy. Catalina must've put something in the tea.

"You go see them and demand they help you get this thing you need to trade for Mateo. They'll do whatever needs to be done after Mateo is safe."

Everything sounded simple. Trying to think about the details, I sighed.

"What do I tell Rosa?"

Catalina lowered me to the slab, and I tried to resist with no success. "I'll tell her about her husband. You sleep."

"I can't. I have to go."

"You'll reopen that wound and bleed to death if you don't let your body rest."

The moment my head touched the slab, though I wanted to stay awake, I conked out. At 9:37am, I opened my eyes in dim, gray light from the window. My display flashed with new messages from Mateo's wife. The system would let me trash them without reading any, but I knew better.

[RosaAcosta: Where's Mateo? He's not answering me.]

[RosaAcosta: If that little prick is seeing another woman, I'll cut his balls off.]

[RosaAcosta: What do I do? Bella, I can't do this on my own. I need Mateo. Get him back for me.]

[RosaAcosta: Bring my man home. Please. Our baby needs his Papa.]

I didn't know what to send. Papa had taught me not

to promise anything I couldn't guarantee.

[IsabellaAcosta: I'll find him.] That part, I knew I could deliver. His condition when I found him...

"Eat something," Catalina called from another room. Plates and utensils tinked and clanked.

Sitting up took more effort than I expected. Panting and sweating, I swung my feet over the side of the slab table and hopped to the floor. My knees buckled, but I caught myself with my fake arm.

If I couldn't even stand, how would I save Mateo?

My coveralls hung from my waist, held in place by the zipper. I spent far too long tying the sleeves around my hips. In the process, I saw the bandage on my left bicep and noticed the injury didn't hurt. Catalina had given me a local.

Using the walls, I staggered into the tiny kitchen. Yellow wallpaper matched the yellow floor, yellow appliances, and yellow ceiling light. Catalina sat at her small yellow table with a cup of coffee in a plain white mug. She'd dressed for the day in a long, purple dress and pinned her hair into a bun. She reminded me of Mama.

The other seat at the table had a plate full of food. Like everyone else in the barrio, Catalina had soy-based pretend food, but hers looked more like real stuff than anything I slapped onto a plate in my shitty little apartment.

I sat and dug into fake eggs, fake bacon, fake orange wedges, and fake cheese with a glass of fake orange juice. Everything had the right balance of protein, vitamins, fiber, carbs, and electrolytes. Any healthy human could survive on this shit.

Once, Mama splurged and got us a pint of real strawberries from a farm collective. They tasted like heaven. Then we went back to hell and ate our slop because we had no other choice. I remembered Papa complaining for a month that she'd spoiled us.

Thinking about my parents made me think about my brother, which led to thinking about Mateo. Too many dead people littered my memories already.

"Stop it, Bella." Catalina set down her coffee. I'd always suspected she could read minds, and she'd never done anything to prove me wrong. "You're just going to panic again. Now is not the time for panic. Now is the time for anger. I know you have plenty of that in your belly. Eat, then go see the gang. They're supposed to protect all of us, and they failed. Tell Big Chimi to his face."

The food tasted like any other soy slop, and I inhaled the rest to get it down as fast as possible. As I set down my empty cup, my heart sped and my foot started tapping on the floor. My fake arm jittered. I wanted to jump to my feet and race around the building a few times.

Catalina set two autoinjectors on the table. Each had a plastic reservoir the size of my pinky finger, filled with bright blue liquid. "I dosed your juice. Take one of these no earlier than two this afternoon. Don't take the second if you can avoid it."

I stared at the two vials. West America regulated the fuck out of stim juice. One hundred people had died from their hearts exploding before someone decided to pay attention. Then they paid a lot of attention.

"Where did you get this shit?"

She raised an eyebrow.

I knew better than to ask questions like that. Stim juice came from the same place she got her other medical supplies. Duh.

"Sorry. Never mind." I stood. Everything worked like it should, unlike fifteen minutes earlier. "Thank you."

"Not before two." She pushed the autoinjectors across the table. "Later is better."

Nodding, I took them and stuck them in a pocket. I had some yelling to do.

CHAPTER 4

Mead First occupied an abandoned bank and warehouse at the intersection of South Mead Street and First Avenue South. The two buildings, connected by an amateur-built tunnel, housed a sizable gang and their shit, plus all their vehicles and guns. Boards covered every window and door on the bank.

Poor slobs, rejected by the gang but with nowhere else to go, camped in the parking lot. Genuine tents mingled with tarp, rock, and cardboard pseudo-structures. Barrels on the edges collected rainwater from a complex set of plastic pipes and funnels. Those folks survived on Processed Food Product, which didn't even try to pretend at being food.

Light rain fell, damping the stench of unwashed humanity. By the time I reached the front door, my hair hung thick and damp.

Instead of a doorbell, the gang had a crank. I turned

the crank, which clicked with gears until it provided power for a light inside. On the few occasions I'd come, I'd never waited long for an answer at the door. Big Chimi probably made the new recruits stand watch at all hours.

Thirty-two seconds later, time I spent reminding myself I'd come to yell at someone, the door opened. Some kid I'd never seen before poked his too-young head out like an idiot. I could've crushed his brains like a watermelon with the door if I wanted. Lucky for him, I didn't.

"Whatchuwant?" The kid's voice hadn't changed yet. He reminded me of a street kid in a sob story vid.

I grabbed the door and yanked it open. Shoving the kid aside, I stormed into the open room full of old couches and chairs. Light came from an arrangement of metal plates reflecting the weak sunshine from skylights on the upper floor

"Where the fuck is Big Chimi?" I screamed into the building.

Kids sprang from the cushions. At least a dozen teenagers cocked and pointed guns at me. They all wore baggy clothes in a dazzling array of faded colors, with a wide variety of patches.

Unperturbed, I planted my cybered fist on my hip.

Moving my injured arm seemed like a bad idea or I would've done the same with it.

"Big Chimi, get your ass down here now!"

One kid broke into a run for the stairs.

Another holstered his gun and showed me both empty hands. This kid, I knew. Kip had been with the gang for years. He had to have hit his early twenties by now. "Hi, Bella. Nice morning, huh?"

With his response, the rest of the guns disappeared and the tension flowed out of the room.

"Don't." I jabbed my finger at him. "I'm not leaving without seeing Big Chimi."

"Yeah, I got that." He beckoned for me to follow him to the stairs. "I'll take you up."

I stalked through the room, my boots clomping on the dull tile floor. The kids decided to ignore me as not a threat, which seemed stupid. Big Chimi didn't have as tight a grip on his gang as he used to, or maybe they'd gotten lazy. Considering the reason I came, the latter seemed likely.

We stomped up the narrow stair formed by odd-shaped metal and concrete pieces. The second floor had dividers, offering privacy to the select few at the top.

Big Chimi stepped through an open door with his

arms raised to deliver a hug and a big smile on his bearded face. His merry girth filled the hallway. I wanted to slap him.

"Bella!" He lunged and wrapped his arms around me. Squeezing enough to cut off my breath, he lifted me off the ground. "I'm so glad you came." He spoke English with a light Mexican accent. Unlike half of his gang, Big Chimi was a barrio boy.

"Put me down," I gasped.

He set me on the ground and let go with an indulgent grin. "You make the building brighter, *amiga*."

I doubled over and sucked in air. My arm throbbed. "You fucked up, you fucking fuck."

Chuckling like I'd told a grand joke, he said, "That's our Bella. Full of fire and spice."

The assholes around us followed his lead and laughed at me.

"You said you'd protect us," I spat as I straightened. "You promised."

Big Chimi's smile faded. "We do protect you. What's wrong?"

"Some assholes came to the garage and took Mateo, you sonofabitch. They want a cow chip from a cop car or they're going to kill him." I jabbed a finger into his chest.

24

"This is your fault. Fuck you if you think you deserve anything else from me."

His face fell into a distressed frown. At least I'd slapped him with words. "What's a cow chip?"

I wanted to sneer at him, but most people didn't know. Telling him might help. After taking a moment to stifle the urge to murder him, I explained. "Momentum Operations Override module. It's the little box that lets them ignore the navbuoys in the flight lanes and change the lights on the ground. All emergency-type vehicles have one, but they want one from a cop car. They must send out a different signal than ambulance ones or something."

Stroking his beard, Big Chimi made a "hmmm" noise. "So that would be valuable."

"Of course it's fucking valuable," I snapped. "But I don't have one and I can't get one. You let these assholes onto *your turf*, making this your problem. Do something about it or I'm going to lead a revolt against your fucking gang."

We stared at each other. The soul of a killer swam beneath Big Chimi's jolly fat man exterior. He'd been thinner and angrier when he first rose above the seething masses. I remembered watching the last rumble before Mead First solidified their claim on the neighborhood. It had happened in the street outside my window. Big Chimi—then, just Chimi—had waded through the rival gang with a fucking machete while his loyal bangers watched over him with machine guns.

Despite all that, he still owed me for Diego's death. My brother shouldn't have died that night two years ago, and Big Chimi knew it.

He raised his hands. "Okay, settle down." Big Chimi beckoned for me to follow him deeper into the labyrinth of the second floor. "Let's sit down and figure this out."

"There's no time to sit and have tea, or whatever the fuck you want to do. I only have until midnight to deliver."

Big Chimi offered me a hand like a chivalrous gentleman. "If my people are going to fix this, we need a plan. Since it's your nephew, and I doubt any of my people have a clue what a cow chip looks like, let alone how to get one out of a car, I expect you to be involved. Come figure this out with me. Please."

I admit the addition of "please" cooled my temper a lot.

CHAPTER 5

Big Chimi, two of his lieutenants, and I sat in huge, cushy chairs facing each other. They all seemed serious, which I found gratifying.

Fagin, a tall, skinny dude with greasy hair and missing teeth, sat on Big Chimi's left. He had the unenviable job of keeping track of all their kids. Whenever Big Chimi needed bodies to do things, Fagin knew which ones to send.

On Big Chimi's right, a curvy black woman held a tablet capable of projecting holograms. I knew Vagabond from before she joined the gang, as a lively, vivacious girl who'd wanted to save the world. She'd settled for saving this small corner of it. Her drive and ambition, cut by real life, had made her Big Chimi's right-hand man.

His third lieutenant's absence chafed. Big Chimi should've called all hands to help with this. "Where's Wardog?" I asked. That *cabrón* had been a pain in the ass until Mateo and Rosa got married. Rosa never said, but I suspected he'd attacked her at some point. I hadn't seen him since I chased him away from the wedding.

"Wardog?" Big Chimi shrugged. "He got out of DeeSeat about a year ago."

That explained why he'd disappeared from my radar. It also told me I hadn't been paying attention to gang politics. Maybe I needed to start.

Something to worry about tomorrow.

"The problem," I said, "is that I don't know exactly where the cow chip is in a cop car. It might be a five minute extract, or I might need five hours."

"Can we get the schematics?' Big Chimi asked.

Fagin shrugged. "This is cop stuff. We don't have anyone who can hack anything that secure."

"Stealing the cop car would be easier," Vagabond said.

"But pointless," Big Chimi said. "They'll disable everything in that car and come looking as soon as they discover it's stolen. That's why we don't steal cop cars."

Vagabond smirked. "That, and cops don't come down here, so there's no access."

"Right." Fagin sighed and rubbed his temples. "We'll have to stage something outside our turf, keep a cop distracted for however long Bella needs to extract the chip, and then get rid of the cop without killing him. The last part is the hardest. I think we could pull it off with a crew of, oh, fifteen, probably."

I shook my head. "As soon as the cop leaves the ground, the flight lanes will snap him into place. He'll notice the chip is gone within five minutes."

Fagin rubbed his eyes with his long, thin fingers. Vagabond frowned and tapped her thumb against her thigh. Big Chimi glared at his hands, laced over his belly.

"So we're all clear," Big Chimi said, "what do you know about these guys?"

"There were two. They wore blacked-out helmets and the one who spoke used a voice modulator. I didn't see what they rode in and out, and the only thing I could say for sure is both are men in decent shape."

"Pros," Vagabond spat. "Messing around on our turf without paying respect."

"Do we really need to get the chip?" Fagin asked. "We can just set up at the meet and kill them both."

I nodded because I wanted to see that.

Vagabond snorted. "If they're pro, they'll think of that. How about mocking up a chip, though? One that's good enough to pass on sight. Once the exchange is made, who cares if they discover it's fake? They want to bring it to us, we can take them no matter what they've got."

"Bring it?" I leaned toward them, wanting to find a way to make this plan work. No, I wanted to save Mateo and didn't care what that took. Killing those two assholes would make me happy, but I didn't need happy. I wouldn't die for a lack of happy. No one survived in DeeSeat if they couldn't handle scraping by with the bare minimum.

"They won't bring it to you," I said. "They'll bring it to me and Mateo."

Big Chimi nodded. "We could set up the garage to repel a couple of assholes."

"What if they have a way to check the chip?" Fagin asked. "If they're smart, they won't release Mateo until they know they have the real deal."

"We're back to needing to pinch one," Vagabond said. "Are we sure we give a shit if the cops deactivate it? Did they say it had to be active?"

"Yes." I cursed myself for bringing that up when those assholes had guns pointed at us. If only I hadn't said anything. If only those fuckers hadn't picked us. "Why did they pick us?" I murmured.

"An excellent question," Big Chimi said. "There are other mechanic shops. Other people who do what you do. Some of them aren't even far away. They picked you, and they did it for reason. That suggests they know you or your nephew, and think you're capable of this task."

"They offered money at first. I told them to fuck off. That's when they took Mateo."

Big Chimi stroked his beard. "Then they see you as their only option, which is interesting."

So these two assholes had picked our garage because they wanted me, specifically, to do their little job. If they'd wanted Mateo, they wouldn't have nabbed him. Unless they wanted him to do something in the meantime, which I could see as possible. Maybe it had less to do with me and more to do with our family.

"People like Bella," Vagabond said. "They respect her almost as much as they respect the Curandera. Her whole family, really. A lot of folks were upset about Diego."

"This could be a move against us," Big Chimi said with a sagely nod.

I narrowed my eyes. "This isn't about you."

"No, of course not. But consider this. If one of the most prominent families in the 'hood is vulnerable under our care, then everyone is. Maybe..." Big Chimi grimaced with a complicated mash of distaste, guilt, and shame. "Maybe you're right, Bella. We've grown lazy, letting our rep do the work when we should be out there, taking care of business."

Fagin clenched his whole body and crossed his arms. "We're not lazy."

Big Chimi shrugged. "Then we're incompetent. But we're going to solve that problem. I want a new patrol rotation, one that covers everything we claim, twenty-four seven. Kids get paired with experienced members."

"We don't have—"

With a slash of his hand through the air, Big Chimi silenced Fagin. "I don't care. This is what we signed on for. If we can't do it, then we might as well give up and let someone else handle the 'hood. But we're not going to do that, because these are our people, and the other gangs in the area are full of assholes."

Fagin and Vagabond looked away. I nodded my satisfaction to him. The neighborhood needed Mead First because the cops didn't patrol around here. I preferred it that way, and a lot of folks felt the same. At least a dozen gangs had come and gone before Chimi stepped up and staked his claim. He'd given us stability and predictability. Anything they did to make my home safer, I supported.

"Now, Bella still has an immediate problem. For a lot of reasons, we want to help Bella. First, you have a one week extension on that chop job. Second, are there any other ways to get one of those chip things besides chopping one out of a cop car?"

I blinked. "I...don't know. I'm not sure if they're installed during manufacturing or added by the cops after delivery."

"I'll find out," Vagabond said. She let her head rest against the cushion of her seat and closed her eyes. The pose suggested she used her implant link to search for the information. I wished her luck, because I didn't know where to begin for that.

"Fagin, I want you to come up with a plan to get Bella access to a cop car that we can feel like won't be driven until...say, noon on Friday at the earliest. If Vagabond turns up another way, this still might be our easier option."

Fagin nodded, though he didn't meet Big Chimi's gaze. I had a feeling a shakeup in the gang's leadership might happen. Not that I cared how it happened. So long as I got Mateo back, they could kill each other to hell and back.

Big Chimi smiled at me. "If you want to, you're

welcome to stay here until we have a plan."

I needed to do something. I also needed to heal. My arm didn't hurt, but it would when the stim juice wore off in another three hours. At least I didn't have to worry about needing to do three hits in one day. No way could these gangers come up with a plan before dark.

Mateo's other employees had probably shown up for work anyway. They needed supervising. When the juice wore off, I'd take a nap.

"I'm going back to the garage." I stood. "Message me when your people are ready to go. Midnight is our deadline, don't forget that."

Big Chimi stood with me and offered to escort me. "We'll get him back."

I turned him down and walked away because I didn't want to listen to more promises he might not be able to keep. The prospect of another unwanted, bone-crushing hug didn't help.

CHAPTER 6

Mateo's four other employees—two cousins and two family friends—all wanted to know why Mateo hadn't stuck around after opening up the shop before any of them arrived. I hadn't locked the doors when I left to reach the Curandera.

I lied to them. Without remorse. According to me, Mateo had caved to Rosa and would stay home for a few days. They didn't need to worry about something they had no ability to affect. And that blood on my coveralls? Nah, just some grease that collected dirt. Never mind the ragged hole.

While they worked on the cars for paying customers, I attacked the chop job. Sure, we had a deadline extension. But I had energy from that fucking stim juice hit and needed to feel like I did something productive for Mateo.

The juice wore off. In the middle of removing the last seat adjustment motor assembly, my arm started to ache. Within a minute, the ache turned to throbbing, then I had to sit. My entire body sagged.

Of course, as I huddled on the floor, hiding from my coworkers, a pile of dirty rags burst into the garage. Under that heap of crap, young, bright eyes scanned the space and locked onto me.

The kid rushed in and crouched by my side at 13:53. Metallic dirt and rotten fruit assaulted my nose. "Vagabond said no dice. We got a target," the kid whispered. "Crew is ready to go."

"That was fast," I rasped.

"What's wrong with you?"

I shook my head and fumbled in my pocket for one of the autoinjectors. Catalina said to wait until two. One-fifty-five was close enough. Keeping the damned thing as low profile as possible, I shoved my sleeve out of the way, pressed it against my arm, and pushed the button. The device made a tiny puff noise and I felt a tiny flicker of pressure.

The kid's eyes widened. "Can I have that?" A dirt-smudged finger pointed at the used autoinjector.

Like I cared. With a nod, I offered it my open palm. The stim juice spread up and down my arm as a cold tingle. It pushed against my pain like a cloud swallowing the sun. I felt it slither up my shoulder and across my chest. Then it hit my heart and I needed to get up and do something.

Reverent awe in their eyes, the kid examined the autoinjector. "Do you have any idea how useful this is?"

"Yes." My voice gained strength with the rest of me. Stim juice—the wonder drug that works fucking miracles.

Grinning, the kid tucked the autoinjector somewhere in the folds of their clothing. "C'mon. Everyone is waiting."

I followed the kid to the door. On my way out, I told my coworkers I'd return in a few hours. None of them would panic if I took longer.

Outside, Kip waited with a group of nine more kids of varying size, all sitting on bicycles. Kip leaned against a hoverbike with parts in five different colors. Lucky for him, they made those out of plastic, so he didn't have to worry about rust.

The ragpile kid ran to the group and snatched the one extra bike. Kip waved for the kids to go. They launched into motion, moving as a double-file armada of pedal-powered obedience.

Kip patted the seat of his bike. "You ride with me." He cocked his head to one side and appeared to check out as much of my ass as possible from the front. "Don't you need tools?"

I held up my cyberarm. "Got it covered." A car as new and shiny as a police cruiser wouldn't need any old-fashioned or non-standard tools like that chop job.

"Nice." He climbed onto the parked hoverbike and flipped the switch to start the engine. Like all hover vehicles, it took a second or two to access his implant and verify his permissions, then the engine sputtered into life. The thing needed a tune-up.

"Do you store this bike outside? It sounds like shit." I climbed onto the bike behind him and grabbed two fistfuls of his denim jacket.

Kip snorted and raised the landing struts. "How much you want to fix it up?"

Like anyone from Mead First would pay me money to do anything. "Cover us for a month."

"I'll talk to Big Chimi."

"You do that."

Kip snapped goggles over his eyes and put on a ballcap. We skimmed the street, two feet off the asphalt, and took the First Street Bridge across the Duwamish Waterway.

The east bank looked abandoned, with weeds growing several feet high across the expanse of broken concrete and rusted steel. At night, the area swarmed with smugglers and black marketeers. Dead bodies turned up there all the time. On the west bank, legit cargo came through a thriving port.

Halfway across the bridge, flying camera drones buzzed overhead. We took the first exit. I stopped watching the world speed past. As I leaned my forehead against Kip's back, my brain chose to replay the moment I'd lost Mateo, prodding for ways I could've prevented it.

We could've taken the job for money. Had I not blown off their offer, though, how would I have found a cop car? There would've been no reason to involve Mead First.

Had they targeted us as a shot across Big Chimi's bow? They could've tried other mechanics first and found no one willing to take on their absurd job. Maybe we'd been the first they could count on not calling the cops, or their last resort.

Maybe they'd never intended to pay us. The offer of money might've been a bluff. In that case, I'd been set up. They must have known I'd have more luck getting a chip than Mateo.

A lot of the options pointed to these assholes knowing us.

Kip stopped the bike under the bright, perky blue

lights of a Ponto de Xadrez convenience store and dropped the landing strut. "We walk from here." The engine coughed and sputtered to death.

"Where are we?" This PdX had no bars on the windows and the camera drones stayed high, so I knew we'd crossed a fair distance.

"Roxhill." Kip offered me a gallant hand to hop off the bike. "There's a house a few blocks from here. The cop living there is on vacation. She's coming back Saturday, so the cruiser parked in her driveway shouldn't move before then. The squirt squad is setting up a distraction to give you some time with eyes focused elsewhere."

I stared at him. "How the fuck did you guys find all that out?"

Kip grinned. "She posted about it on her public profile. Husband surprised her with an anniversary trip to some beach in Baja. They'll be back Saturday."

We walked down the street together. I prayed to God for this to go smoothly. For Mateo's sake.

CHAPTER 7

Roxhill seemed like a place where decent, ordinary people lived. Low picket fences marked the boundaries of yards with toys, bicycles, dogs, and gardens. No windows had bars or boards. Instead of drones, it had cameras mounted on the streetlights. Paint blared in bright, cheerful colors. I saw no cracks in the sidewalk, and all the trees bore vibrant green leaves. Even under gray skies threatening rain at any moment, the area felt cheerful and friendly.

Kip paused at a bus stop and sat on the sheltered bench. Unmarked plastic walls surrounded it on three sides. No one had even drawn on the shelter with a marker, or scratched anything into the plastic. He patted the spot beside him.

I stood in front of him, wishing I could cross my arms. "We don't have time to sit around."

He smirked and set his hands on my hips. I raised a

hand to slap him. The purr of hovercar engines passing behind us kept me from doing it. People—regular people who knew nothing of DeeSeat and its fringes—could see us.

"Play along so we fit in a little."

Glaring at him, I ignored the obvious problem of my dirty coveralls. I fit into this neighborhood as well as a dog in a flock of geese. "Get your hands off me."

"We have to wait for our distraction, so give me five minutes of pretending we're a normal couple, a little down on our luck, waiting for a bus."

"If you try to kiss or grope me, I'll knee you in the balls."

A shadow of distress crossed his face, and he squeezed his legs close around mine. At least I knew he believed me. "I'll keep that in mind."

The whirr of bicycles zoomed past. We both turned to look. Our armada disappeared around the next corner. Small bells clanged in the distance. I started to take a step to follow them, but Kip held me in place.

"Wait. One more minute."

I didn't believe we had to wait, but said nothing. Aside from touching me, he hadn't done anything.

When my clock indicated that one minute had

passed, Kip let go and stood. "Can I ask you a personal question?"

"No."

He took the hand of my injured arm with a laugh. "I'm just wondering why—"

"None of your business." I had a suspicion about what he wanted to know. Everyone always wanted to know why I hadn't gotten married. Everyone except Diego, who never gave a shit, and Catalina, who already knew the answer.

"The arm scares guys off, I bet." He led me up the street. We followed the path the bicycle armada had taken.

I didn't respond. The arm was the reason, but not like he thought. Those memories all sucked. Focusing on the reason I'd come and what I had to do kept me from falling into that black hole.

"I don't think it's scary," Kip said.

"Fuck off," I snapped. It'd be a cold day in Hell before I considered fucking a gang member.

In the middle of a block filled with more American Dream houses, a cop cruiser sat in a driveway. Three houses further, on the other side of the street, the bicycle brigade played a noisy game in someone's driveway. It involved a lot of shouting and bouncing. The nearby cameras all pointed at them.

Kip and I strolled down the street, watching the game. We needed to fit in, after all. I had no need to fake my confusion at it, because I had no idea what they were doing. The game probably had rules, but the kids moved like a throng of chaos.

Shrubbery screened the cop's front door from the street, which made it easy for us to pretend like we meant to visit. Kip tugged on my arm, sending a sharp, stabbing pain through it, and we crouched on the front walk. He retrieved a small box from his jacket pocket.

Once, many years ago, I'd seen an override switch. The garage didn't service vehicles with that kind of tech, so we had no legal justification to own one. That Mead First had one explained how they jacked so many different kinds of cars.

Kip pressed a button and turned the small dial, click by click. The device cycled through different options for simulating the handshake with the car's computer brain so we didn't need the cop's implant present to open the door.

Despite my irritation with Kip, I appreciated his presence. On my own, assuming I could've found the car in the first place, I would've reached this point and not known what to do. Like I'd told those masked assholes, I fix cars, not steal them.

"It's not working," Kip muttered. "It always works. Why isn't it working?" He smacked the box.

I stifled the urge to swipe it from him and try it myself, but he'd probably used it five hundred times before. His experience beat mine.

"What's plan B?"

"There is no plan B. Plan A was supposed to work."

I covered my eyes to avoid strangling him. There had to be another way to get this fucking chip. "Can you break the window?"

"Not without setting off the alarm. That kind of defeats the point."

"Okay." I would not fail Mateo. "We're going to breathe for a few seconds." My advice seemed sound. After three deep breaths, I opened my eyes and stared at the house's front door. The fake wood door and its shiny brass handle offered no distractions, giving me a chance to think in peace.

Police vehicles got maintenance, so they had an override. Kip's module didn't have the right thing to interact with it. Mateo needed me to come up with another option. I knew how to remove a bumper, open a hover port, and remove the undercarriage protector. Any of those three would gain me access to some parts of the car's guts, but probably not the right parts.

Kip kept fussing with his box. The kids kept playing their game. I rubbed my temples, trying to think.

The front door opened. A man wearing sweatpants and a t-shirt printed with "SPD" in large, block letters stood on the threshold with a steaming mug in one hand. His skin had the light brown of a single Native or Latinx ancestor a few generations back.

Kip rabbited.

I froze.

CHAPTER 8

The man watched Kip abandon me. "Hi."

I stared at him like a moron. My mouth opened and shut.

He approached and crouched beside me, his brown eyes on my sleeve and its blood stain. Fresh, real coffee taunted my nose. Did he eat real food? Probably not all the time. Only rich folks did that. Real coffee, though...

"Are you okay?" He seemed nice. Pleasant. Friendly. Honest. I couldn't put my finger on why, those things just filled the air around him, like a strange sort of cologne.

"No," I whispered, not sure what else to say.

"There was a lot of noise out here until a moment ago. Is that how you got hurt?"

Not trusting myself to speak, I shook my head.

"What's your name?"

Nothing bad came from telling him that. Any cop

could use their scanner to access my implant account. "Bella."

"Hello, Bella. My name is Nate. What brings you to my door today?"

His door. "Aren't you supposed to be on vacation with your wife?"

He raised his brow. "You stopped by when you thought I wouldn't be here?"

Glancing to the side, I thought I could escape.

Nate shifted to the side before I moved, blocking the path. "I won't hurt you, Bella. Would you like to come inside and talk?"

I blinked at him. "What?"

He smiled at me. Warmth reached his eyes. "Let's talk about what's bothering you." He held out a hand to me. "I've got more coffee."

In all my years, I'd never met anyone outside of family who'd treated me like this. Nate asked for nothing while offering me something. I didn't think he'd arrest me unless I tried to assault him.

Wait.

"Are you a cop?"

"Yes, but not a patrol officer. The car is my wife's."

"Is she here?"

His smile faded. "No. She's actually on vacation. Bella, I promise you're in no danger from me. Or my wife. Please, come inside and have some coffee with me."

I didn't know what to do. Never before had I been in this kind of situation. All my usual bravado wilted outside my home turf. Maybe I belonged in my barrio and should never have left it. I thought of Mateo bleeding to death in the stadium parking lot because those two assholes wanted something I couldn't deliver.

"Why?"

He stood, still offering his hand. "I believe things happen for a reason."

Nate seemed so sincere. I took his hand and let him help me stand, then escort me inside his house.

He led me through a spartan, white and beige house to the kitchen. No pictures hung on the walls. Everything about the place reminded me of furniture store ads. It all had that bland, purposefully arranged yet never occupied feel.

In the huge kitchen, I found signs of humanity. Dishes from a breakfast for one littered the sink and stovetop. They had a fridge alongside their soycase, with an animated screen image of the happy couple. Nate held his arm around an attractive blonde woman with paler skin and blue eyes.

They smiled and waved from a table at a restaurant on the water. I recognized the Olympic Mountains in the background, so it must've been someplace in Seattle overlooking the Sound.

"Our first anniversary," Nate said with a smile. "Married a decade now."

"Congratulations." I sat on a stool at the bar hanging from the back of the island in the center of the room. "She seems..." I didn't know what word to fit there. The vid gave the impression of a serious person forced to do something fun against her will and not enjoying it. "Nice."

Nate fetched a porcelain mug like his own and poured coffee from a glass carafe. He chuckled. "That's not the word most people use."

I spread the fingers of my fake hand over the surface of the bar, wondering if they'd sprung for solid stone, or only a thin layer over plastic. How did two cops afford all this?

Coffee placed under my nose banished all thoughts.

"Do you take cream or sugar?"

Instead of answering, I picked up the cup and inhaled the aroma. This felt like strawberries. I imagined this asshole having the gall to offer me real cream from a real cow.

As I took my first sip, I heard a machine clunk and

whirr. The sound took me off-guard and made me jump. Even more startling, Nate swore. Though I'd only known him for five minutes, I'd already gotten the impression he didn't know how to use those words.

"What was that?" I pictured a robotic thing alerted to the presence of an intruder and coming to throw me out at knifepoint.

Nate hurried around the island. "Nothing. Stay here." He disappeared through the doorway.

"Nate, who's here?" a woman asked. Another clunk and whirr echoed off the walls.

I stared at the empty space, blinking.

"No one," Nate said. "Go back to bed."

Curiosity pushed me off the stool and to the doorway. Nate bent over the woman in the vid as she tried to crawl across the floor with one mechanical leg half-disassembled. A panel on her face hung open, exposing the complex machinery under her realistic skin. Another panel on her bare back also lay open.

As I watched, fascinated and revolted by the sight of a man trying to wrangle his sexbot, I noticed she wore no clothing at all. Thanks to that detail, I could tell she had no sex parts. Bare skin covered the space between her legs with no holes of any kind. Her small, perky breasts had no nipples.

"There you are," the woman said, meeting my gaze. Her eyes, including the one bare in its socket, seemed so real and alive. "Nate, you're being rude. Introduce us."

Nate looked up, saw me, and swore again. "Greta, you're not fit for company right now. You're supposed to be sleeping."

"What kind of...um..." I trailed off, not sure if Greta would take offense and attack me for calling her anything other than human.

"That's hardly an introduction." Greta reached her hand for me. "Hello, miss. I'm Greta."

"Bella," I said, still not sure how to react. The frustration on Nate's face, though, moved me to try to help. "Nice to meet you, Greta. I just need Nate's help for a little bit with a...with a..."

"A neighborhood thing," Nate said. He wrangled the squirming bot and pressed something on her back.

Greta fell limp and inert.

"Thank God," Nate huffed. He raked a hand through his hair and looked to me. "Please go back to the kitchen and pretend you never saw this."

As if I would ever obey a command like that.

CHAPTER 9

I approached and knelt beside Greta, examining her leg. "This is amazing. Is she fully robotic with no human parts at all? Where did you get the AI? Did you know the servo here is broken?"

Nate hefted Greta over his shoulder in a fireman's carry. "What do you know about broken servos?"

I took the question as an invitation and followed down the hall. "I'm an auto mechanic. Certified for almost everything on the roads and in the flight lanes."

He brought us to a room at the end of the hall with no windows and set Greta into a frame that could hold her at any angle. I helped him straighten her limbs and secure them.

When I pictured bot workshops, nothing like this place came to mind. I thought of huge factory floors with robotic arms holding things and doing a lot of the work, giant computer screens with VR access, and parts and tools everywhere. Nate's workshop fit the rest of his house—neat, spartan, and beige. Aside from Greta's plassteel frame, anchored to the floor and ceiling, he had two tablets and a workstation with a cable ending in an old-fashioned brainjack plug.

"Maybe you can help me, then. I'm not a roboticist. I'm an AI programmer. She gets tweaks once a year, and this round's upload had some...unexpected effects."

I furrowed my brow at him. "You're faking being married to an android and going on vacation every year for your anniversary to cover up the fact you're updating her programming?"

He sighed, and I had my answer. "Can you fix the servo or not?"

"Why would you go to this much trouble for an android?"

"Because." Nate ground his teeth. "She's a cop."

"You got her into the police academy and she passed without anyone noticing? Wow. That's some hard-core AI —"

"No." Nate huffed and pointed to the leg. "The Seattle Police hired me to be her overseer. Can you fix the servo or do I need to call in the damage? If I do, Greta will probably be ordered to arrest you, and you'll be convicted on falsified evidence to keep anyone from believing you when you try to reveal that androids are part of the police force."

I stared at him and blinked. This feeling of diving into a pool much deeper than I wanted kept happening, and I didn't like it. Catalina had told me to find the fire in my belly if I wanted to save Mateo.

Digging deep, I found it under all the confusion and fear. I jabbed my finger at his chest. "Are you threatening me?"

"Yes." He smacked my hand aside. "Because I can't begin to imagine what kind of illegal activities brought an auto mechanic and a bunch of ragged kids to my door. But I'll point out that I did notice your friend had his attention on the cruiser in the driveway, which leads me to suspect all kinds of interesting things."

"Fuck you," I spat. The urge to turn my back on him and walk away surged in my blood so hard that my arm throbbed. The pain made me clutch the wound and stagger. The stim juice couldn't have worn off already. Not yet. The first hit lasted about three and a half hours. This one still had another two and a half hours to go.

Nate caught me. He scooped me into his arms and

carried me into a different bland room, this one with a bed. "I showed you mine, now you show me yours."

As if I could stop him. I cringed while he yanked down the zipper on my coveralls and pulled my arm free.

"This needs a fresh bandage," he murmured.

While he ran out and fetched supplies, I stared at the texture on the ceiling around the gold-edged light fixture. Imagine having light anytime, day or not, without having to run on the treadmill or pour alcohol into the generator reservoir. On demand. And real coffee.

Fuck, my arm hurt. I didn't think the juice had worn off, because I didn't feel tired or worn, but the anesthetic effect had.

Nate hurried into the room carrying a genuine first aid kit, complete with the words and a red cross printed on the side. He dragged a chair to my side and sat. "Tell me what you wanted to steal from the cruiser."

Sonofabitch. I groaned while he peeled off the bandage.

He frowned at what he found beneath. "This is a fresh gunshot wound. How are you walking around?"

"I live in DeeSeat."

"That's not an answer." He poured something onto a

gauze pad and pressed it to the wound.

It hurt. I screamed. Gasping for breath, I wheezed, "Is this an interrogation?"

Nate smirked. "Not intentionally. Answer the questions anyway."

Despite not wanting to say anything, I had nothing to lose. So far, I hadn't done anything illegal that he could prove. Him knowing my plan didn't equate to him foiling it. Besides, the plan had gone to hell anyway. We'd have to find one someplace else. With luck, Kip or a message from him had already made it home and reported on our failure, and Vagabond already searched for a new target.

"I need an active cop cow chip to save my nephew's life. Some assholes took him and won't let him go until I deliver one."

He nodded with the explanation as though it didn't surprise him. "What are they going to do with the chip?"

"I don't know. We didn't sit down and have a friendly chat. They shot me to prove they're serious."

"And who were those kids?"

"Local gang."

Nate sprayed synthaskin over the wound. It burned and froze at the same time. "You're an auto mechanic in a gang?"

"No. We pay them protection. I convinced them to help me."

His gaze flicked down the length of my body and he smirked. "You must have some interesting skills for persuasion."

"Go fuck yourself," I snapped as I turned my back on him and sat up. "I wouldn't touch any of those shits for more money than they all have, put together."

"Ah." He cleaned up his kit.

"Do you have any painkillers?" My arm didn't want to cooperate enough to go back into my sleeve, so I pulled off the other one and struggled with tying them around my waist again.

"Yes, and I'll give you some as soon as you fix that servo, and anything else you find wrong with Greta."

Sonofabitch. "Fine." Determined to get through this shit, I lurched to my feet and used the wall for support to get back to his workshop.

He followed, his arms out to catch me if I fell, the asshole. "It occurs to me that, if the SPD had certain, very specific knowledge about the disposition of a certain, very specific cow chip, they might be able to track and apprehend certain, very specific men."

I stopped at the workshop doorway. "I fix your android and you help me take the cow chip?"

"I doubt my or Greta's superiors would consider this a good plan, but what they don't know..."

"How are you going to keep them from arresting me for stealing it in the first place?"

Nate huffed. "I can't. That'll have to be up to you and your gang friends."

Great. Relying on Mead First had done me so much good so far, how could doing it again possibly go wrong? Still, I didn't have any other options, and Mateo didn't have forever.

I nodded. "Deal."

CHAPTER 10

[IsabellaAcosta: Can you please have someone inform Big Chimi that I'm going to need a pickup in a few hours at the location where Kip abandoned me?]

[CatalinaAcosta: I should be able to deliver that message for you, *chica*.]

[IsabellaAcosta: Thank you.]

Like many folks in the barrio, I'd avoided handing over my commcode to anyone in the gang. Once they could contact you, they could nudge you. One nudge here, another nudge there, and pretty soon, you joined the gang without realizing it.

Kneeling beside Greta, I touched her flesh. Somehow, they'd made it feel like human skin. Then again, they'd given me the power of touch through chrome, so maybe it wasn't that amazing after all.

"She's incredible," Nate said. "When I joined the

program, I had no idea they'd come this far in replicating human appearance. That skin is made from a plastic polymer. It doesn't sweat, but otherwise, you can't tell the difference."

"Do you fuck her?" I prodded the broken servo, checking the damage to see if I could weld it or it needed a new part.

Nate coughed. "No." Glancing at him, I saw that his cheeks and nose had darkened. "The marriage thing is all pretend. Her programming includes a backstory about why we have a sexless relationship and why she's fine with it."

The servo needed one piece replaced, and a whole lot of realignment. Great. "Why not make yourself her brother?"

"It was part of the project parameters. They wanted it this way so no one thinks she's available and tries to date her."

I retracted my finger shell in favor of my power drill. "Sounds good for her, but shitty for you."

"Oh. Uh." He blushed again. "I don't really... Hey, I never seen tool attachments in a hand like that before."

If he didn't want to talk about it, neither did I. "Custom job."

Nate moved to the seat in front of the workstation and tapped the screen. "How long have you had it?"

Dark memories flickered in their corner, waiting for a

moment of weakness. "About two decades."

He stared at me longer than I considered polite. I suspected he wanted to say something about my age, but couldn't decide how to word it.

"I didn't think they'd figured out how to shrink that kind of rig that long ago."

Nice save, Nate. "The hand is only about three years old." Two years, ten months, three weeks, and two days. The replacement had happened two weeks before my brother's death. "The original wasn't as useful."

"Ah."

My power drill whirred in the awkward silence. I disassembled the servo and laid out the parts in sequential order, like I did with any unfamiliar job. Halfway through, Nate connected the plug to the access panel in Greta's back.

When I stood to find a replacement part, Nate pointed to drawers. I opened one and found small boxes, each labeled with a part name, number, and schematic.

Nate cleared his throat. "Can I ask how you wound up with a fake arm?"

"You can ask anything you want," I said. My tone, I thought, suggested against that particular line of inquiry.

"How did it happen?"

I scowled. "None of your fucking business."

"I guess losing your whole arm would be pretty unpleasant, yeah. Sorry."

"Losing my arm wasn't the bad part." The box I needed was in the third drawer I tried because Nate had organized them alphabetically, and I didn't know the name of the broken part. He had five of them.

"Sure. I can see that. They can replace an arm."

"Yeah." Breath, hot and rancid, blasted across my neck and shoulder. The intense memory made me shiver. I dropped the box, scattering the parts across the floor.

Nate hopped out of his seat to help me collect them. "Are you okay?"

"I'm fine." The cyberhand didn't shake, at least. It didn't do shit like that. Lose its grip momentarily, yes. Shake, no.

My cheek remembered the feel of concrete. I covered my eyes, not wanting to hear that voice echo in my head.

"Bella?"

I jumped. My heart pounded in my chest. Nate. Greta. Robot cop. Workshop. Fixing a servo. Replacing a part.

Nate crouched beside me, holding the box. He

watched me with concern so real I almost mistook his brown eyes for Papa's.

"You're not fine." He touched my knee.

I flinched from him and took the box. "Fuck you." The sooner I fixed the fucking servo, the sooner I could leave to save Mateo.

As I knelt to deal with the servo, I felt Nate's gaze on my back. Ignoring it took effort. Pry out the broken piece. Mount new piece. Replace the other pieces I'd removed.

"Did he go to jail?"

My hand slipped and I dropped a different piece of the servo. "What?"

"The man who hurt you. Did he go to jail?"

"I never said—"

"There are more ways to say things than with words."

I wanted to get up and walk away. Those two assholes taking Mateo shouldn't have cost me this much. They didn't get to take this much from me.

"Bella, I promise I won't hurt you." He stuck his open hand into my line of sight, holding a PainTab sealed in its blister pack.

No one did nice things for nothing. When he'd withheld it before, that had made sense. Giving it now didn't.

My arm hurt, or I would've turned it down.

The PainTab dissolved on my tongue, leaving blissful numbing in its wake. As it smothered the ache, I wondered if I'd made a mistake mixing it with stim juice. Too late to fix that, but at least I'd know the cause if something weird happened.

"No," I said. Nate deserved an answer for his small kindness. "He didn't go to jail."

"Why not?"

"Because he was a cop." The old echo of his rough, calloused hands on my skin made me want to vomit.

Nate said nothing while I focused on my work. I'd spent enough time dealing with my old pain that none of it should've caused me a problem. The foreign environment, I decided, along with the time pressure, the injury, and the fact I sat with a stranger, fixing a cop robot, had brought this to the forefront.

Those two assholes had a lot piling up on their tab.

"This was twenty years ago?"

Great. Nate had probably looked it up to find out what happened. At least that spared me from having to explain the worst parts.

"Yes, it's the cop who was cleared of all wrongdoing

and then Ferdinand Acosta killed him outside the courthouse and ten cops opened fire. Nobody remembers the cop's name because he was innocent." The flat monotone of my voice surprised me.

Nate sucked in a breath. "Oh my God, he dropped an *engine block* on your arm? And they let him walk?"

"They said that part was accidental."

My mind flashed to the garage that night. Accident, my ass. Malicious glee fit the expression on his face a thousand times better. With a low growl in the back of my throat, I shoved it all aside. Mateo needed me. I had no time for this shit.

I tucked the last piece into place. "The rest, they dismissed for lack of evidence."

"That's horrifying."

"I don't know why you're surprised. No one saw it happen. The word of a poor, teenage Latina counts a lot less than a white cop's."

He went quiet again. I glanced over and saw genuine shock and distress plain on his face. This guy had no idea what happened in the real world. Nate spent all his time safe inside his walls, his gender, his job, and his whiteness. If this had nothing to do with me or mine, I would've laughed at him.

"That's life in the barrio." I tightened the last screw and checked Greta's knee motion. "This is fixed." The ordeal had taken time, and I only had an hour and a half before I crashed again.

Nate stared at the floor like he needed to think too hard to do anything else.

Part of me wanted to let him indulge his confusion. The rest of me had no idea how long I needed with his car. "I did my part. It's your turn."

He jumped like I'd hit him. "What?"

"Car. I need access to the cruiser outside. You promised."

"Oh. Right." Nate seemed genuinely shaken, as if he'd never heard about a cop doing something wrong and getting away with it. He stood and led me down the hallway to the front door. "When is the trade going down?"

"Midnight."

We stepped outside. The sky had cleared and everything sparkled in the sunshine like a rain shower had passed through. Nate and I both shielded our eyes from the unexpected brightness.

"Do you need me to start the engine?"

"No. Pop the hood and unlock the front doors."

The hood clunked. Nate sat on the front stoop to watch. I avoided touching him as I passed. Under the hood, I found a more advanced engine compartment than I'd ever seen before. Mead First never jacked anything newer than about two decades old, because around that time, car companies had done drastic redesigns that made the parts a lot less valuable. Despite being a hovercar, that Ford in the shop still had a transmission and radiator.

This thing had stuff I'd never seen before. Nothing had labels, warnings, or arrows. Instead of curved and angled things that fit together like a jigsaw puzzle, I saw an array of identical rectangular boxes. The cruiser didn't even have a windshield wiper fluid reservoir. At least, not one I could identify. Maybe the fancy windows vibrated themselves clean, or something ridiculous like that.

Fortunately, I knew what a cow chip looked like. Unfortunately, I didn't see it. Leaning over the compartment, I prodded things to see if they reacted enough to give me a hint about their purpose. One had to be the engine. Probably. Unless the engine was mounted in the back. I didn't think they'd do that for a cop car, considering they put prisoners in that part.

"What's wrong?" Nate asked.

"Nothing."

He'd already told me didn't know anything about mechanical workings. Explaining the problem to him meant wasting my time. Speaking of time, I had about one hour and fifteen minutes before my second dose of stim juice wore off.

None of the boxes wiggled or revealed their secrets. I abandoned the engine compartment in favor of the front seat. Sliding into the driver's seat of a cop cruiser made me feel... It smelled like pine air freshener. Where the passenger seat should have been, the car had a weapons rack with a collection of guns in different sizes. A wall of clear plastic separated the front section from the back.

Power. This car felt like power. I put my hands on the dashboard where the steering wheel would pop out when Greta deactivated the autopilot. With this car, she could go anywhere, anytime. The flight lanes didn't constrain her, and neither did stoplights. New cars ran on solar cells you couldn't see, so they could go forever.

Taking this thing would give me an edge when meeting those two assholes. I had guns, I had a way to scare the shit out of them, and I had a way to escape. My hand touched the closest gun.

I remembered the barrel of a gun pressed to my temple. I remembered gunshots on the courthouse steps. I remembered the thump of a bullet in my arm.

"Any luck?" Nate appeared in the space left by the open door.

He startled me. I snatched my hand close. My brain scrambled for coherence. The car required an authorized implant to drive, and Kip had proven this thing couldn't be boosted. Without Nate or Greta along for the ride, I had no way to take the car. So I needed to get my shit together, find the chip, and get the fuck out.

"I'm still looking, thanks." I examined the covers on the dashboard, looking for a release. They had to have access to the parts underneath for repair and replacement.

"Ah. Look, um, I'm sorry about what happened to you and your family. And I appreciate you not hating me from the start because of it."

I snorted at him, trying to bury everything again. "Were you even born twenty years ago?"

He smirked. "Yes. I was in middle school."

I grunted. Somehow, he managed to stay naïve for thirty-some years. Keeping his head buried in virtual reality and AI crap had probably been a big help for that.

Running my fingers over the edges of the dash, I found a divot. Retracting the cover on my middle finger revealed a plassteel wedge that expanded for use as a chisel. I showed Nate, flipping him off in the process, and dug it into the divot.

"What would you consider justice for that?"

"Justice?"

The cover popped free. Underneath, I found a collection of smaller boxes, each as anonymous as those under the hood. How cop mechanics did their job mystified me. Maybe they had to use scanners. How shitty to have to scan every single thing to find the one you need.

"There must be something I can do to help you find closure."

"Closure?" I stared at him and had no idea what the fuck he thought he could do. "What planet are you from?"

"Sorry, what?"

"What fucking planet do you live on? The one I know doesn't have closure or justice. It has shit that happens and you suck it up and deal or it eats you up and shits you out."

He leaned toward me like something stupid in his dumbass head made him think I needed a hug. My left arm still didn't work, so I couldn't stuff a hand in his face.

"Don't touch me," I snapped.

Nate froze. "I just—"

"I don't care."

"But I—"

"None of this," I growled, "is about you. Leave me the fuck alone so I can save my nephew's life."

He sighed and let his shoulders droop. "I want to help you."

"I don't need your help, I just need the fucking chip."

"That's not what I meant."

"It's what you said."

I turned away from him to examine components in the dash. The first one I tried to wiggle popped out. The boxes each had a port, and the dash had a row of chips to plug into them. Fucking computers. Internal combustion engines were messy, loud, and complicated, but at least they made sense.

"I could give you some money."

For a moment, I thought I'd heard him wrong. Someone like him offered money to someone like me for a few specific reasons, and charity wasn't usually one of them. As I slid the box back into place, I tried to imagine what kind of demented fantasy played in his head.

On second thought, I didn't want to know.

"No, thanks." I popped out another box and checked behind it.

"There must be something I can do for you."

I snorted and kept checking behind the boxes. "Are you going to have me arrested?"

"No, of course not." He seemed so scandalized by the idea that I had to restrain myself from laughing in his face.

"There. You're doing something for me. Pat yourself on the back. Double your effort by not interrupting me anymore so I can work."

"That doesn't seem fair. Compared to what you've gone through, I mean."

"What does that even mean? I don't want your fucking pity. You want to do something about it?" I stood, getting into his personal space, forcing him to take a step back, and jabbing him in the chest with a chrome finger. "You're a cop. Do something about cops from the inside."

He stumbled a step and blinked at me.

I didn't let him talk. "One guy destroyed my arm and raped me, but he was never the problem. The entire police department stood behind him. The district attorney's office flubbed the prosecution. The judge threw out evidence that would've convicted him. The jury decided he was telling the truth and I was a hysterical girl who lied. You want to fix something? Fix that shit. Teach those motherfuckers they can't just do whatever they want and get away with it."

"I...I don't know how."

"Yeah? I don't know how to find a fucking cow chip in a fucking cop car, but I'm here, doing my goddamned best." I turned my back on him and slid into the car again. Out of the corner of my eye, I saw him stagger to his front stoop and sit like he'd been punched in the gut. In a way, I supposed he had.

The clock in my vision kept ticking. I pulled every box in the dash to check behind them and found nothing. As I fitted the cover back into place, I wondered if they'd put something like this under the seat. If the car had a glove box, I would've expected to find it there, but it didn't.

I backed out of the car and checked under the seat. Behind the front frame bar, I saw a box. My hand didn't fit through the small gap. The attachment inside my pinky finger, though, did. Designed to fish for loose screws, a thin, telescoping rod extended eighteen inches from my fingertip. At the tip, it had a tiny electromagnet.

With the tip, I found a button that released the box's lid. And there it was. Alongside three other chip slotted into four ports, the cow chip waited for me to extract it. Using the finger rod took some effort, but I'd had a lot of practice using it in unconventional ways.

My clock claimed I had about half an hour left on my stim juice hit when I straightened with the chip in hand. I slammed the car door shut and did Nate the courtesy of dropping the hood.

He still sat on his front stoop, his head in his heads. I pitied him. Every time I looked at my arm, I remembered why I had it, but my life had been that way for twenty years. He'd just learned he was complicit in a cycle of systemic abuse that had ruined lives and killed people.

I leaned against the wall beside him and had an urge to pat his shoulder. He didn't deserve that. Not yet. Maybe in a few months, he would.

"Thanks for letting me take this. After midnight, this thing should be in the hands of the guys who took Mateo, and I should have Mateo back. Until then, please don't report this. After that, do whatever you want." I declined to point out that I knew where he lived, and I had a gang full of people willing to kill at my disposal. He could figure that out on his own.

Nate looked up, his eyes wide and blank. "I wish..."

"Wishes don't solve problems. Good luck, Nate. Stay decent." I walked away.

Kip met me on his hovercycle at the end of the street without looking at me. He stared at the road while I climbed on the back. I could feel the juice ebbing, so I said nothing. Big Chimi had probably said some choice words to him already. I doubted anything positive would happen from me piling on more.

By the time we rolled to a stop in front of the garage, I knew I'd reached the end of my second high for the day. Lifting my leg to get off the bike took too much effort. I shambled to the door and leaned against the wall. Someone had locked up the shop. As I'd expected, no one worried about me. They'd all gone home and the last one out had closed for the night.

The rattle and clunk of Kip's hovercycle faded into the distance, leaving me alone. My strength evaporated. I slid down the wall as the sun disappeared behind buildings. In a heap on the dirty concrete, I wondered if five hours would give my body enough downtime to handle the third dose of stim juice.

My eyelids drooped. How would I get to the stadium? I had no idea. Big Chimi hadn't said anything about taking me there. Kip hadn't said anything at all. If I had to walk, I'd need some time. I set an alarm through my implant to wake me at eleven.

Though I tried to stand so I could go sleep in my apartment, I passed out.

CHAPTER 11

I awoke to the sensation of my entire skull buzzing. My body felt leaden and stiff, my arm ached, and my head throbbed. Silencing my alarm only fixed the buzzing problem, and I had to fight to stay awake. Rolling onto my side didn't help, so I kept going until I sat with my back against the wall.

Mateo needed me. I checked the cow chip, then fished the second autoinjector out of my pocket and used it. Like before, surging heat spread from the injection site on my arm. When it hit my heart, I felt an electric blow to my chest. I gasped for breath and thought something might explode.

No dying tonight. Hopping to my feet, I pushed off the wall and fell into a jog. Every part of my body—except my lungs, of course—wanted to race farther and faster than I knew I should. Restraining myself to a slow run took effort.

Darkness kept me from paying attention to anything

alongside the road as I jogged up Fourth Avenue. No one sane wandered at these hours without a weapon. Except me, of course. I heard a man scream in agony across the street and kept going. Protecting us fell to Mead First, and if they couldn't handle it, I sure couldn't. If they caused it, I could do even less.

Strings of colored lights threaded through the railing for the bridge over the train tracks flashed, allowing me to see a crack in the sidewalk before tripping over it. Trains blew their horns one after another, proving they didn't give a shit where they ran. Camera drones followed the trains, keeping them free of trouble.

I remembered one incident several years ago when some guys tried to hijack a train. Five units of SWAT had swooped in and rained death and terror on the area for twelve hours. They'd miraculously missed hitting the train, its tracks, or the road while killing all the hijackers and destroying every building bordering the rails. No one had ever produced an official tally for the dead from that night.

And no one had fucked with the trains since.

Running past, I wished I could jump on one and ride it north. Four more miles to the stadium lot. Warehouses to either side had been repurposed into living spaces. The gas station to the left still operated, with gas brought by rail. My cousin's wife's family owned it. Farther up the street, I passed a collection of small markets full of crap everyone needed but no one wanted.

The area became less Latinx and more white trash. Somewhere in here, Mead First gave way to a gang called Nightmares. They hated us, and we hated them, though I couldn't say why. The color of our skin, the fact we spoke Spanish, our accent, whatever. For all I knew, they'd decided to hate us because we weren't them.

Not that it mattered.

I took an eastbound cross-street to First Avenue, knowing everyone regarded that street as a kind of neutral territory. Sort of. Tourists on that road tended to get robbed like anywhere else, but if you moved with purpose and confidence, no one bothered you. Most of the time.

With every footfall, I thought of Mateo and those two assholes. I didn't care what they did with the cow chip, so long as they let my nephew go. Maybe Nate would stick to his word and have them arrested. Maybe Mead First would show. Maybe it would become a giant clusterfuck of monumental proportions.

Halfway there, and with a half hour to go, I slowed to

pick my way through debris and catch my breath. My vision hyperfocused on sharp shadows thrown by tiny things and distant light. I missed the big things and ran into a wall, smacking my wounded arm, which sent a jolt of pain through me.

"Hey, Princess. C'mere. I'll make that feel better." I didn't recognize the voice or see its owner. He sounded large and creepy.

Instead of answering, I picked up my pace. Don't acknowledge them and they let you pass. I tucked my arms close and jumped over a block of concrete to put obstacles between us. My heart thumped in my ears.

The return trip with Mateo, whose condition I didn't know, seemed impossible, but we'd manage. Somehow. After dealing with so much shit today, no trip through Nightmare turf would stop us.

Someone stepped into my path. I crashed into the shadow. We fell. He cushioned my impact and grunted.

"Jesus Christ, Bella," a man said with a groan. "What the fuck?"

I scrambled to the side and onto my feet, ignoring my arm and ready to run. The guy's voice sounded familiar, though. "Kip?"

"Yeah. Big Chimi sent me to get you to the exchange on time. I've been looking all over the place for you." He grunted as he stood.

"Like I expected you to show up," I growled. Turning my back on him, I marched up the street.

"Bella, it's not safe here." His boots clomped on concrete, then I heard the clunk and grumble of his hoverbike. My blood had been pounding in my ears too much to hear its approach. He followed me. "Let me give you a ride. You'll never make it on foot."

"Fuck you," I snapped at this snot-nosed punk who thought he knew something I didn't.

Kip sighed loud enough to hear over his bike's engine. "I'm sorry I ran, Bella. I thought you were right behind me. When you weren't, I didn't know what to do, so I went back to base. I didn't have your commcode and no way in fuck was I going to break into a cop's house."

I stopped and looked over my shoulder. Every minute we hung around here increased our chances of attracting Nightmares.

"And I should've punched him in the face," Kip said. "Then we could've either run for it and figured out something else, or used his implant to access the car."

Did I accomplish anything by staying mad at Kip? Not really. "You should've taken me home instead of to the garage," I grumbled as I stepped around the bike and climbed on the back.

My cyberarm jolted with a spasm. Thanks, stim juice.

Kip didn't answer. He revved the bike and plunged through the darkness. I decided to assume his goggles had a night vision enhancement. The alternative meant trusting him to know these streets well enough not to crash in the pitchy darkness.

I didn't trust him.

CHAPTER 12

We reached the old stadium complex, which everyone regarded as neutral turf. Deals of all kinds happened here. On any given day or night, someone traded something out of sight of drones and cops—weapons, information, people, whatever.

Huge chunks of concrete littered the area, pieces fallen from both arenas. Long strings of lights powered by chained solar panels decorated the buildings. The asshole pair hadn't said which part of the parking lot to wait in, so Kip chose a spot with a wide view.

Fifteen minutes to midnight, I stepped off Kip's shitty hovercycle. He pushed his goggles onto his forehead.

I had so much energy that I bounced and my cyberarm spasmed.

"Relax," Kip said. "You're going to wear yourself out like that."

"Shut up," I snapped.

"Look, Bella. I said I was sorry. I meant it. If it hadn't been a cop—"

"Shut up," I said again. "It's fine. I'm on stim juice."

Kip stared at me. "Jesus. Why?"

"They shot me. I'd be on the ground otherwise." I pointed to the hole in my coverall sleeve.

He gaped. His mouth moved with no sound, making him look like a fish. "Why the fuck didn't you tell anyone they shot you? Fuck, Bella, I would've brought a crew if I'd known that!" He stepped off the bike and popped open the seat. "That means they're fine with shooting you, which means they're fine with killing you. And probably me and Mateo."

I furrowed my brow and tried to understand his logic. The words zipped in one ear and out the other without pausing. "Why the fuck would you think they wouldn't kill us all?"

Kip pulled two pistols out of the seat and offered one to me. "Big Chimi said they're probably just fucking with us. They wouldn't kill you to fuck with us. They'd need you scared of them so you'll do what they want."

Waving off the gun, I tried again to understand his

point and couldn't focus on it. "I don't know how to shoot."

"They don't know that." Kip put the gun in my cyberhand and aimed it at the ground. "Point this part at an asshole, flip this switch, brace for recoil, and squeeze the trigger. Try not to flinch."

The gun felt awkward and heavy in my hand, like a kluged tool I expected to fall apart in the middle of use. I stuffed it in my pocket. Flinching seemed inevitable, especially if it knocked out my ears again.

As if he'd heard my thoughts, Kip retrieved a pair of foam earplugs. I still had mine from twenty-four hours ago, and stuffed them into my ears. They put a dent in the noise without making us deaf.

Kip shoved his bike behind a chunk of concrete and hid behind it. "Stay where they can see you, and don't look at me. I'm your secret weapon."

"Right," I muttered. Picking a different block of concrete to lean against, I tried to relax. This would work. Mateo would go home to his wife and baby tonight. I'd sleep for the next day.

Purring engines drew my attention. Two lights danced over the asphalt until they blazed in my face. I raised my fake arm to shield my eyes. They'd destroyed my night vision, probably on purpose.

Before they reached me, they stopped. Two small engines shut off. They'd ridden hoverbikes. Thankfully, the lights shut off with the bikes.

"Do you have a cow chip?" Asshole number one still used a voice modulator.

My vision adjusted, and I only saw two figures. "Do you have Mateo?"

One asshole waved to the other, who tossed a body off the back of his bike. I couldn't tell if it was Mateo or not, or if he was alive. They wouldn't have killed him, though. That would've been stupid. Right?

Pulse speeding again, I tasted bile at the thought of dragging Mateo's corpse home.

The man on the ground groaned.

"He's alive," the asshole said. He sounded like he snickered.

These fucking fucks. All traces of fear swirling in my gut drowned in anger. "Prove it!"

"Show the chip!"

I dug the chip out of my pocket and held it up. "If Mateo can't walk under his own power, I'll smash it."

Both men brandished guns. The talky guy pointed

his barrel at me. Asshole number two pointed his gun at Mateo. I didn't trust Kip with these odds, but I didn't fucking care. If Mateo couldn't walk, these sonsofbitches didn't get to leave happy.

"If you smash it, we'll kill you both."

"Then I guess you better hope he can walk, *pendejo*. Otherwise you wind up with nothing but two dead bodies." I could almost hear Papa sighing and Diego cheering my bravado.

We all glared at each other.

Like Big Chimi, this asshole looked away first.

"That's right," I snarled. "Don't you fuck with with me, *chiquito*."

The asshole turned to face me again. While his partner used a boot to nudge Mateo, the asshole stalked toward me.

"I'm not a little boy," he growled.

Standing my ground, I held the chip behind me and thought about flinging it for distance. That would keep these assholes busy while I dove for Mateo. Then I had another thought and circled to the side, trying to get closer to Mateo.

As far as I could tell, the asshole focused on me and didn't notice how I turned us so I backed toward the bikes and he followed.

Behind him, Kip popped up and pointed his gun. Between one of my steps and the next, he fired. The asshole staggered. His partner jumped and swung his gun to point at Kip. I ran for Mateo.

Gunshots roared behind me. Pain flared in my thigh. The leg buckled. Stim juice still pumping through me, I rolled until I shielded Mateo with my body.

The second guy pounced on me. His elbow jarred my jaw. I saw stars and dropped the chip. He scooped it off the ground.

"I got it!" He leaped at his bike, abandoning and ignoring me. "Let's go!"

I surged to my foot, intending to throw my body at him. Instead, the first asshole tackled me. We fell together over Mateo, making him groan.

A hoverbike engine buzzed to life, clean and powerful.

The asshole and I wrestled. He squeezed the wound in my leg. I screamed and banged my fake elbow against his helmet. The face plate cracked.

He tried to point his gun at me. I pinned his arm with my shoulder. The gun fired next to my head. Even through the earplugs, I heard ringing. Rage beyond reason filled me, and I smashed my elbow against his face plate again. It cracked deeper.

I dug my fingers into the crack and ripped the helmet off his head.

His eyes widened.

Kip kicked the gun out of his hand and pointed his own weapon at the asshole's face. "Stop now or you die."

Stunned, I watched Wardog raise his hands. He looked the same as I remembered.

"Bella," Kip said, "I got this fucker. Check Mateo."

Yes. Check Mateo. I scrambled to my nephew's side and found a growing pool of blood. He twitched. I rolled him onto his back. His mouth moved and he gurgled. The blood came from a ragged hole at the base of his neck, where it met his shoulder.

"Ssh," I heard myself say. I grabbed the hole like I could stop the bleeding with my one hand. "You're going to be okay." Tears rolled down my cheeks.

He faded before my eyes, his life seeping out around my chrome fingers. His body subsided and deflated.

My nephew died.

I sat on my feet, unable to feel anything but that old,

aching void ripped open and spilling fresh blood. My father, my mother, my aunts and uncles, my brother—everyone killed by guns in this fucking shithole. I could leave, but where would I go? How could I abandon the last of my family?

Wiping my face didn't stop the tears.

"You killed him," Kip growled.

Looking up, I thought he meant me. But he bared his teeth and pressed the barrel of his gun against Wardog's neck.

Wardog said nothing. He lay still, aside from breathing.

Breathing. Something Mateo would never do again. His son would grow up without a Papa. His wife lost her husband.

A growl built in the back of my throat. I stuffed my hand in my pocket and wrapped my chrome fingers around the gun. My leg ached and I didn't care.

"You fucking killed Mateo Acosta, you moronic prick," Kip said.

I'd never killed anyone or fired a gun before. Cool, hard metal in my hand, I raised my arm. Like Kip had said, point this part at the asshole.

Wardog saw me. Kip followed his frightened line of

sight and saw me. They watched me flip the switch.

"Bella." Kip kept his gun on Wardog while leaning out of my way. "Gang's on their way. We'll take care of this for you."

Without taking my sight off Wardog, I braced for recoil. "Like you took care of Diego?"

"You know we did everything we could for him."

"The fuck you did!"

I remembered finding Diego's severed head on the garage doorstep. Their version of doing "everything they could" had amounted to cleaning up the head, finding his body, helping us bury him, and killing the guys who did it.

"You should've protected us in the first place. Big Chimi acts like everything was fine until yesterday. Someone should've been there when they took Diego for my unpaid medical bills. Someone should've protected Rosa from this fuck, and someone should've been there when he rolled back into the barrio. No more! No fucking more of this shit. If you can't handle the job, I fucking will."

I squeezed the trigger. The bullet missed Wardog's head by an inch. He screamed and rolled to the side. Kip dove out of the way. I moved my arm and fired again. Wardog stopped screaming.

Swinging the gun to the side, I aimed at Kip. I'd just killed a man and I felt nothing. Killing Kip wouldn't bother me either. I knew it with certainty as cold and hard as the gun itself. In that moment, I could've murdered the entire gang with no remorse.

"You tell Big Chimi I'm done waiting for him to do his fucking job. What's left of my family will defend ourselves with or without his help."

"Please don't shoot me." Kip held up his hands in surrender. "I'm not your enemy."

"You're not my friend, either." I lowered the gun and made myself look at Wardog. The bullet had gone into the back of his head at the base of his neck and burst out through his forehead. Bits of bone and brain decorated the ground in a cone-like spray.

This fuck had probably picked us because he'd nursed some kind of flame for Rosa and convinced himself he only needed to prove himself to her. We'd thought it had to do with gang politics or something like that. No. Just another asshole trying to prove himself the better man to some woman who didn't want him.

"Bella. I…I'm sorry for…this." Kip sounded quiet and pathetic.

"You're always sorry about the shit that happens. Try stepping up and not having anything to be sorry for."

He looked down. "I'll get him home," he said. "I promise."

I hurt everywhere. Tears rolled down my cheeks. Snot dribbled from my nose. Blood covered my hands and leg. Static filled my head. The stim juice kept me going for now. If I didn't get attention soon, I'd bleed out and none of this would matter.

"You're damned right you fucking will," I snapped.

CHAPTER 13

Though I'd intended to march home, my body failed me. I couldn't even get off the ground. A Mead First armada, led by Vagabond, descended upon us. Kip explained what had happened, omitting nothing. Vagabond gave Mateo an honor guard, and Kip took me to Catalina. Somewhere along the way, I passed out in his arms.

Soft light greeted me at 9:37am. I lay on Catalina's slab again, this time without my coveralls. I wore my tank top, underwear, and socks. By turning my head, I could see a bandage taped to my thigh. The synthaskin Nate had applied remained in place.

"Aunt Catalina?" I didn't even try to get up.

Plastic scraped across plastic and Catalina entered the room. She'd dressed for the day in black. "Everybody knows what happened," she said with a serious frown as she stepped to my side. "We almost lost you too."

The previous day crashed over me. Catalina held me and we cried together. Whenever I got enough strength for it, I'd go see Rosa. Maybe we'd cry together too, or maybe she'd scream at me. For the moment, I mourned my nephew.

When I stopped weeping, Catalina wiped my face, sat by my side, and held my real hand. She helped me drink warm, minty tea.

"Big Chimi came to see you," Catalina said after a long silence. "I told him to come back for lunch."

"You should've told him to go fuck himself."

"He promised to help Rosa."

Big Chimi and I would have a chat about what "help" meant in this case. If he thought I wanted more gang activity in our barrio, he was wrong. We needed something better. Something different. Something that protected everyone, all the time, not just whenever a ganger happened to stroll past.

We needed real cops, but I didn't want them either. No one in or near DeeSeat did. Everyone had a reason. Our family had been here from the beginning and had made a life for ourselves. Too many forces had conspired to take it away.

Time to fight back. And fuck anyone who got in my way.

Other Books by the Author

Darkside Seattle
Street Doc
Fixer
Mechanic
Hacker (coming 2018)

as Lee French
Maze Beset trilogy
superheroes in denim
Dragons In Pieces
Dragons In Chains
Dragons In Flight

Spirit Knights series
young adult urban fantasy
Girls Can't Be Knights
Backyard Dragons
Ethereal Entanglements
Ghost is the New Normal
Boys Can't Be Witches

Tales of Ilauris
sword & sorcery fantasy
Damsel In Distress
Shadow & Spice
Al-Kabar

The Greatest Sin series
epic snark fantasy
co-authored with Erik Kort
The Fallen
Harbinger
Moon Shades
Illusive Echoes
A Curse of Memories

Anthologies
Into the Woods: a fantasy anthology
Merely This and Nothing More: Poe Goes Punk
Unnatural Dragons: a science fiction anthology
Missing Pieces VII
Artifact
What We've Unlearned: English Class Goes Punk
Bridges (editor)
Undercurrents
Hideous Progeny: Horror Goes Punk
Enter the Aftermath

Non-fiction
co-authored with Jeffrey Cook
Working the Table: An Indie Author's Guide to Conventions

About the Author

L.E. French is the cyberpunk pseudonym of Lee French, a fantasy and superhero author. She lives in Olympia, WA with two kids, two bicycles, and too much stuff. An avid gamer, compulsive writer, and casual cyclist, she can often be found on myth-weavers.com, sitting in her BeanBag of Inspiration +4, or riding her bike around the city.

She is an active member of the Northwest Independent Writers Association, the Pacific Northwest Writers Association, the Science Fiction and Fantasy Writers of America, and the Olympia Area Writers Coop, as well as being one of two Municipal Liaisons for the NaNoWriMo Olympia region.

Thank you for reading! If you enjoyed this book, please consider posting a review wherever you buy your books.

87999568R00067

Made in the USA
Columbia, SC
30 January 2018